Blast to the Past™

Blast to the Past™

Ben Franklin's Fame

By Stacia Deutsch & Rhody Cohon

Illustrated by Guy Francis

ALADDIN PAPERBACKS

New York London Toronto Sydney

With love to Carol Kantor,
aunt and business builder.
Special thanks to Nathan Sigars for
the conversation and the muscles.
—Stacia

To my gal pals:
Allison, Liz, and Claire
—Rhody

ALADDIN PAPERBACKS
An imprint of Simon & Schuster Children's Publishing Division
1230 Avenue of the Americas, New York, NY 10020

Designed by Lisa Vega
The text of this book was set in Minion.
Manufactured in the United States of America
First Aladdin Paperbacks edition October 2006
2 4 6 8 10 9 7 5 3 1
The Library of Congress Control Number 2006921955
ISBN-13: 978-1-4169-1804-2
ISBN-10: 1-4169-1804-3

Contents

PROLOGUE
Time Travel

IF YOU SAID TO ME, "HEY, ABIGAIL! WHAT'S YOUR favorite thing in the whole world?" I would have to answer, "History Club."

History Club is way better than hanging out and watching TV. Better than swimming. Even better than eating double chocolate chip ice cream.

On Mondays, after school, our third-grade social studies teacher, Mr. Caruthers, sends three of my friends and me on a mission back in time. Jacob, his twin brother Zack, Bo, and I call our top-secret time-travel adventures "History Club."

And our teacher, Mr. Caruthers, is so super cool, we call him "Mr. C."

But, there is this evil woman named Babs Magee.

She used to be Mr. C's assistant. Then one day, she stole a time-travel computer that Mr. C invented in his laboratory under the school gym. Now, she's popping around history, visiting important people on a list of names that Mr. C made.

Babs Magee wants to be famous. But she doesn't want to work for it. She'd rather just steal other people's inventions or ideas. She figures if she can get a historic person to quit their dreams she can do whatever that person was meant to do. She wants to get into our American history books and have everyone talk about "the Amazing Babs Magee."

It's a lame way to get famous.

When Mr. C discovered that people on his list of American historic figures were quitting, he knew he needed to set history straight. But since he is too busy working on a new invention, he asked Bo, Jacob, Zack, and me to help him out. It is our job to go back into time and convince those famous Americans not to give up their dreams.

Mr. C gave us a brand-new time-travel computer. It looks like a hand-held video game with a larger screen and extra buttons. When we put a special cartridge in the back, a glowing green hole opens and we jump through time. Taking the cartridge out brings us home again.

We have two hours to get the task done. We've never asked what happens after the time limit is up. I hope we never find out.

So far, we've been really lucky. On all our adventures, Jacob, Zack, Bo, and I have managed to keep history on track. We've foiled Babs Magee's schemes. And landed back at school with seconds to spare.

Today is Monday. I can hardly wait for school to end and History Club to begin.

CHAPTER ONE
Monday

"WE ARE GOING TO LEARN ABOUT ONE OF THE MOST famous people in American history." Mr. Caruthers, the most amazing social studies teacher on planet Earth, leaned back on the edge of his desk and folded his arms across his chest.

It was 8:05 and Mr. C had just arrived in class. Every Monday Mr. C is late. And totally messy. Today, his hair was sticking up. His suit was a crumpled disaster. And his glasses were falling off his nose.

Mr. C didn't seem to notice his appearance. Or maybe he didn't care. It is part of what made him so cool. Mr. C is super smart and also a little absent-minded.

We didn't used to know why he was late and a mess, but now we do. . . .

Every Monday morning, just before school, Mr. C creates a time-travel cartridge for our History Club meeting. When he seals the lid on the cartridge, there is always a huge explosion. He says the time-travel cartridge doesn't work without the explosion.

Why Mr. C doesn't make the cartridges on a different day, or get up early enough to shower and change clothes afterward, I'll never know. Maybe, like doughnuts, time-travel cartridges are better fresh.

"This American is so famous, everyone recognizes his name," Mr. C said as he pushed up his glasses. "We'll be studying his accomplishments all week."

Usually, whoever Mr. C talks about in class is the same person we visit after school. Of all the kids in the third grade, Mr. C chose just Jacob, Zack, Bo, and me for History Club. The four of us are table partners and we take the responsibility very seriously.

"Who do you think we'll meet today?" I leaned over and whispered to Zack while Mr. C paused to straighten his tie and run his fingers through his hair.

"Hmm," Zack wondered aloud. "Someone so famous, we can talk about him all week . . . Maybe Elvis Presley?" He played a little air guitar and wiggled his knee under the table. "Wouldn't it be rockin' to visit the King?"

"Groovy," I said with a laugh. Zack is the funniest guy I know. And, yeah, it would be cool to visit Elvis, but I didn't think that's who we were studying today.

I looked past Zack to his twin brother Jacob.

Jacob and Zack might look the same, but their personalities are totally opposite. Jacob is neat and clean and organized, whereas Zack is always a wreck.

Today Zack was wearing jeans and a T-shirt, with parts of his breakfast on the front. I could easily recognize syrup and chocolate milk.

"Who do you think Mr. C's talking about?" I asked Jacob.

"Bill Gates would be my guess," Jacob replied.

"He's 'the father of modern computing,' you know." Jacob was wearing khaki pants, and a T-shirt with a computer on the front. He really likes computers.

It was a good idea, but usually we only visit people who have been dead a long time. As far as I know, Bill Gates lives in Seattle.

Bo was sitting the farthest away from me at our table. He was wearing sweatpants and a long-sleeved gray sweatshirt. Bo's real name is Roberto, but we call him Bo for short. I would have asked him who he thought it was, but Mr. C had cleaned himself up and was now pacing in front of the room, lecturing as he walked.

"The man we will be learning about was an inventor, politician, soldier, statesman, poet, ambassador, shopkeeper, bookseller, printer." Mr. C stopped to catch his breath, before adding, "Cartoonist, scientist, journalist, chess player, weight lifter, and he loved to read, too."

Now I was certain it wasn't Elvis or Bill Gates.

"Please get your textbooks," Mr. C instructed. There was a rustling of papers as we all rushed to pull our books out from the little shelves under our desks.

When we were ready, Mr. C said, "Turn to page one-forty-four." He paused, giving us just enough time to find the page number. "There, in the middle of the page, is a picture of an American legend: our famous forefather, Benjamin Franklin."

Mr. C started searching for the correct page in his teacher's guide, when Maxine Wilson's hand flew up in the air. "Excuse me, Mr. C," she interrupted. "There's no picture of Ben Franklin in my book."

Hands were popping up all over the classroom. Everyone was reporting the same thing: Ben Franklin was not in our textbooks.

Mr. C looked down at his teacher's guide. He had a confused look on his face. I could tell that Ben Franklin wasn't in there either.

Khoi Nguyen raised his hand, and then informed him, "There's a painting of some woman in the middle of page one-forty-four."

"That's odd," Mr. C said as he stood tall and slowly wandered toward Khoi's desk. "Just yesterday I reviewed my notes for this morning's class." Mr. C scratched his head then pushed up his glasses. He glanced down at Khoi's book. "I am certain that Ben Franklin is on page one-forty-four."

I looked at my own page 144. I checked the number. And then, double-checked.

It was true. Ben Franklin wasn't there. I studied the painting of the woman. The small sketch was blurry.

In the drawing, the lady's face was half covered by a floppy hat. She was standing next to an old-fashioned printing press, showing a printed document to two men. The woman looked sort of familiar, but I didn't know from where.

I gave up trying to place the woman's face. I turned a few pages in the book to see if Ben Franklin was on page 145 or 244. Knowing Mr. C, it was possible that he wasn't remembering correctly.

Bo, Zack, and Jacob flipped through their books also. We were all looking for Ben Franklin.

Bo loves to read. He's the newest member of our class. The first thing I found out about him was that he reads everything and remembers everything he's ever read.

"Something isn't right," Bo said, rubbing his chin. The second thing I learned about him was that Bo always rubs his chin when he's thinking hard.

Turning to the index in the back of the book, Bo ran one finger down the names, then reported to us, "There's no Ben Franklin in our American history books at all."

One more thing about Bo is that he is shy. Especially around adults. There was no way he was going to announce his discovery to our teacher. But I'm bold and never shy. So I decided to tell Mr. C myself.

I raised my hand and held it there for a second. But when Mr. C didn't call on me immediately, I lowered it again. A thought was trying to break through into my brain.

An important thought.

I looked again at page 144. This time I studied the picture. I read the words under the drawing. When I realized the truth, I raised my hand so fast, the

motion shot me up and out of my chair.

"Mr. C!" I called across the room. He'd given up trying to find Ben Franklin in Khoi's book and for some reason was flipping through the pages of Cindy Cho's history book. I guess he thought the two books were different.

"Be patient, Abigail," he said as he licked his finger and sped through the pages.

I heard Zack laugh and say, "That's like telling an elephant to tiptoe." Zack was being goofy, but he was right. I'm never patient. I try, but it's just too hard.

I was standing near my desk, bouncing on my toes, holding one hand up above my head, waiting for Mr. C to call on me.

While I waited, I happened to look down at Bo. He was carefully reading page 144. His eyes went big like a UFO when he also realized what was going on.

Jacob and Zack were still skimming through their own books searching for Ben Franklin.

"He's not in there," I told them, dropping my hand and coming around the table. I turned Zack's book back to page 144 and placed the textbook between them so they could view the page together.

"Stop looking at the picture. Just read the page, instead. It says right here"—I pointed to the exact words—"'She's the most famous statesman, inventor, and printer in American history!'" I skimmed down the long list of all the things she'd done. "She also enjoyed weight lifting and playing chess."

"Oh, no!" Jacob and Zack groaned at exactly the same time.

"Oh, yes!" I replied in a loud, full voice. "Ben Franklin has been replaced by Babs Magee!"

CHAPTER TWO

The Green Hole

"ABIGAIL"—MR. C PUT HIS FINGER UP TO HIS LIPS—"Shhh. You are making too much noise."

"Sorry," I apologized. "But Mr. C, did you *read* page one-forty-four?"

"Not yet," Mr. C admitted. "I was busy looking for the correct page for Ben Fran—" his voice broke off as he began to read the words from Cindy Cho's book.

Mr. C suddenly announced, "Class dismissed."

"What?" Khoi said, jaw hanging open. "We haven't learned anything yet."

"Go outside for recess," Mr. C told everyone. Then, a little impatiently, he waved his hands at us and added, "Now."

"But, Mr. C, it's not time for recess," Eliana Feinerman argued. She was staring at our teacher as if he had gone nutty.

"Fine." Mr. C swept the papers on his desk into a crumpled pile, preparing to run out of the room. "If you don't want recess, you can go next door to Mrs. Hodgkin's class for an extra period of math."

"No! Please. Not Mrs. Hodgkin. Anyone but Mrs. Hodgkin," Zack whined. "Can't we have more PE? Science? I'd even pick language arts over math."

I cut him off, whispering, "Mellow out, Zack. You, me, Jacob, and Bo aren't going to math. *We* have to help Mr. C." I pointed down to our history book. The picture that seemed fuzzy before was now staring very clearly up at me. Even in the small drawing, I could tell that Babs Magee was wearing her usual yellow hat and matching coat, smiling her sneaky smile.

"Obviously," I said softly to the boys, "Babs Magee won this time. She finally convinced someone to quit. She convinced Ben Franklin!" I reviewed the list of stuff our book said Babs had been: Politician.

Inventor. Visionary. The list went on and on.

She'd taken credit for everything Ben Franklin had done and now, she was known as one of the world's most famous Americans. She finally got the fame she wanted. By stealing Benjamin Franklin's life!

What happened to poor Ben Franklin? I wondered. Where had he gone?

I looked over at Mr. C. His glasses had slipped back down his nose, but he didn't push them up. "Don't move," he told the class, motioning like a traffic cop for everyone to stop. "I'll be right back." Mr. C rushed out of the room.

I heard the door to Mrs. Hodgkin's classroom open. Mr. C's voice echoed in the hallway.

A few seconds later, he came back. "It's all been arranged," Mr. C announced. "A sudden emergency has come up. Today, the entire class will go next door for a double math period." Everyone groaned, even Zack.

I was going to poke Zack, but Jacob did it first. "I don't think Mr. C means *us*," Jacob said.

Suddenly I was full of doubt. Mr. C would want

us to help him put Ben Franklin back into history, wouldn't he? We were going to time-travel, weren't we? Maybe he planned to do it himself. I just assumed he'd want Bo, Zack, Jacob, and me to go. We'd done so well on all our other adventures. Then again, my mom says never assume.

"Abigail, Jacob, Zack, and Bo," Mr. C interrupted my rambling thoughts. He came close to us and whispered, "Stay here while I lead the rest of the class next door."

When the door closed and we were alone in the classroom, I turned to the boys and said confidently, "I knew he'd want our help."

Mr. C stuck his head back in the classroom and told us to hurry. We practically had to jog to keep up as we followed him to the back of the school gym and down the stairs.

"I knew Babs Magee would try to convince Ben Franklin to quit today. He's next on my list of names. I just didn't realize that she'd get this far, this fast." Mr. C took a key from his pocket and opened the wooden door to his laboratory. "I made the time-travel cartridge for you this morning."

I thought about saying, "Duh." I mean, looking at his suit and hair, it was pretty obvious he'd already made the cartridge. It was hard, but I held my tongue.

Mr. C went on. "I was going to give it to you after school, but now we can't waste any time." Mr. C didn't say anything else as he crossed the room. He bent down next to a locked safe and began to press the buttons for the combination.

He took our time-travel computer and a small cartridge from the safe.

"Babs Magee has made a terrible mess of history. Find Ben Franklin and put things back." He held out the computer and cartridge toward Jacob.

Jacob reached out, but suddenly, Mr. C snatched back his own hand. "Maybe I should do this myself," he said, with a distant look in his eyes. "History has already been altered. Fixing it is a huge responsibility. We can only hope Babs hasn't already created mass confusion and that when history is saved, people will immediately forget about her."

Mr. C looked down at the black cartridge in his

hand. "I am also concerned about the danger you might face when you run into Babs Magee."

"Danger?" Zack repeated softly. "What does he mean by danger?" This time, Zack wasn't joking. For all his silliness, Zack also has a healthy heaping of worry. "Today is not a good day to die," he said, tapping his foot wildly. "I have big plans for tomorrow. I'm going to join the Pottery Club."

"That'll only last a few days," Jacob said, and gave his brother an elbow in the ribs. "I mean, last week you were in Musical Theater for two days. And you didn't even make it ten minutes into Chemistry Club before you asked to go to the bathroom and never came back."

"Chemistry Club wasn't my thing," Zack said with a grimace. "All I'm saying is that I can't go around getting killed today. I have things to do tomorrow!"

"No one's getting killed," I reassured Zack.

"Yeah," Jacob said to his brother. "Zack, stop being such a ninny."

"I'm not a ninny," Zack countered. "You are."

Bo must have seen Zack's hand ball into a fist

before I did. He jumped between them, saying softly, "It's not about pottery. It's about history. Do you want Babs Magee to finally win her place by stealing Ben Franklin's fame?"

Zack's fist relaxed. Jacob took a step back. And I turned to Mr. C, saying, "We're ready. We can do this."

"Yeah," Jacob added. "We can handle it."

"Are you sure?" Mr. C lowered his eyelids and looked suspiciously at Jacob and Zack. "There can be no fighting or arguing on this mission." He then looked at each of us in turn. "It will take all of your skills. You'll have to work together."

"We can do it," I said again with confidence. The boys immediately agreed. Jacob and Zack even called an official truce.

"All right," Mr. C said with a nod. "You are searching for the moment when Babs Magee steered Ben Franklin off course." Mr. C was very serious. "If you can get him back onto his life's path, the rest will unfold properly."

Sounded easy to me. Ben Franklin would be back

in our social studies textbooks in no time at all.

Our teacher turned to Bo. "Have you read about Ben Franklin?" Being shy and all, Bo simply nodded. "Biographies? His autobiography?" Mr. C asked. Bo nodded twice, meaning he'd read both types of books. "Good. Your knowledge is going to help a lot on this adventure."

Mr. C handed Jacob the computer and cartridge. "For this mission, you won't need to adjust the settings on the computer. However, the cartridge might need some tweaking." He handed Jacob a small screwdriver. "Open the back panel on the cartridge. You'll know what to do." Then he warned, "Don't take off the lid, though. You don't want the cartridge to explode."

"Explode?" Zack burst out. "You mean Jacob could blow us up?"

Jacob looked concerned, but he said with confidence, "I won't blow us up."

"I trust you," Mr. C said firmly.

"Now, Zack," Mr. C said, and put his arm around Zack's shoulder, "you are the one who needs to

convince Ben Franklin to get his life back on the correct course."

"Why me? Why would he listen to me?" Zack asked, his shoulders growing tight.

"Because you two have a lot in common," Mr. C concluded.

Zack glanced up at Mr. C. "Did he want to be a potter? Tomorrow, I'm going to try Pottery Club, remember?"

"As a matter of fact"—Mr. C smiled, walking over to his workbench—"Ben Franklin did try making ceramics for a while." At that, Zack's shoulders softened and a glint of light passed through his eyes.

"All right, then," Mr. C told us. "You'd better get going. Good-bye and good luck." He leaned over a cardboard box and began sorting purple and orange wires into two piles.

Jacob slipped the cartridge into the back of the computer. The green time-travel hole opened in the middle of the floor. Glowing smoke was slithering like a snake across the cement. Jacob, Zack, and Bo jumped in, one after the other.

I was the only kid left in the laboratory.

"Hey, Mr. C." I was watching the hole carefully so that it didn't close before I jumped. "What about me? How are my skills going to come in handy?"

I am bold and curious. Those are my skills. I wanted to be useful, too.

Mr. C smiled and walked quickly around his workbench. "Good thing you asked. In my hurry to get you kids going, I forgot to give you this." He handed me a small notebook with a slick cover and a matching pencil. "Abigail, you always have a lot of questions," he said. "Think like a detective."

Mr. C pointed at the time-travel hole and said, "You're going to Philadelphia for the signing of the Declaration of Independence. You'll land at Independence Hall, near the Liberty Bell. The boys are already there."

CHAPTER THREE
1776

"HOW COOL IS THAT!?" I SAID. IT WASN'T A QUESTION, but rather a statement made in total awe.

We had landed in a large town square. Standing before us was a tall, three-story, brick building. I guessed that this was Independence Hall, like Mr. C had said. There was a balcony off the front. And a tower on the roof. A huge brass bell hung in the tower. It was the bell that made me exclaim again, "Totally cool!"

I told the boys what Mr. C had said. We were at Independence Hall in Philadelphia and that was the Liberty Bell.

"I'm ahead of you, Abigail," Bo told me. "I've never been here before, but I read about the

Liberty Bell in one of those books on Ben Franklin. He lived near here."

We knew we needed to go find Ben Franklin, but couldn't resist checking out the Liberty Bell for a few more seconds. Nowhere on earth was there another bell like it. The Liberty Bell was the most important bell in United States history.

"Jacob and I came to Philadelphia once with Mom and Dad," Zack said. "The Liberty Bell was in a special building for tourists. We had to stand in line for almost an hour to see it. By the time we got to the front of the line, the dumb bell was cracked. All that waiting to see a broken bell," Zack complained.

I knew Zack was kidding. Not about the wait, but about the crack. Everyone knew that the Liberty Bell was cracked. Seeing the crack was part of the reason people stood in line. It was a really famous crack.

Bo explained, "No one knows for sure when the bell got cracked. Some people think it was in 1846, when it was rung in honor of George Washington's birthday.

Others think the bell cracked a long time before then."

One thing was certain: We were in 1776 and there was no crack in the Liberty Bell. Not yet.

I took a good look around where we were standing. The town square was crowded with people. I could tell something important was about to happen. The air had that electric buzz when people are gathering for a really exciting event. Maybe the bell was about to ring?

I closed my eyes for a second. I could almost hear the booming sound a bell that big would have made. "Cool," I said one more time. I opened my eyes. "It's so awesome to be here for the very first Fourth of July celebration."

"Hey!" Jacob had a puzzled look on his face. "The computer says the date isn't July fourth," he reported. "It's August second, 1776."

"That's weird," I commented.

"The time-travel computer must be broken. We've missed the signing of the Declaration of Independence," Zack muttered. "We'll never find Ben Franklin now."

"No, no. The computer works perfectly," Bo cheered. "We're right on time."

I was really confused about the date. Since I was supposed to be thinking like a detective, I felt like I should be writing stuff down. I pulled out my new notepad and pencil. On a clean piece of paper I wrote the date: August 2, 1776.

"I can explain," Bo began. I wrote down what he said. "You see, the Declaration of Independence was written at a time when America was in a huge fight with Britain. Britain had been controlling the thirteen colonies, but the colonies wanted to rule themselves. While the Revolutionary War was being fought by soldiers in other places, here in Philadelphia, Ben Franklin and four other men were secretly creating a document proclaiming America's freedom."

I was writing so fast, my hand was cramping.

Bo went on. "After many drafts, the Declaration of Independence was completed and voted on by a group of leaders on July second, 1776. These men were called the Second Continental Congress." Bo pointed up at the Liberty Bell. "On July eighth, the

Liberty Bell was rung for freedom. And on August second, 1776, the Declaration of Independence was finally signed by the members of the Continental Congress."

"Well," Jacob said, tucking the computer into his pocket for safekeeping, "that explains why we are here in August." He fanned himself with his hand. "It sure is a hot day."

Zack wrinkled his face until his eyebrows touched each other. "I don't understand. Why do we have barbeques on July fourth instead of August second? And set off fireworks? And march in parades? And—"

"We get your point," Jacob tried to cut him off, but Zack kept on going.

"And go to baseball games? And eat hot dogs and apple pie—" Zack probably would have gone on all day, but Jacob flicked him in the head, saying, "Enough already."

For the second time today, Bo stepped between them. He obviously wasn't going to let them argue anymore. "It says July fourth, 1776, on the top of the Declaration," Bo told the twins. "That's the day it was accepted by Congress and printed, but not the day it was signed."

I took one last look at the Liberty Bell and felt a surge of pride.

We were about to meet the famous Ben Franklin! Maybe we'd even get to see him sign the Declaration of Independence. All we had to do was find him first.

"What does Ben Franklin look like?" I quickly asked Bo.

Bo gave us a description of Ben Franklin. "He was the oldest member of the Second Continental Congress." We were looking for a seventy-year-old man with a round face and a balding head.

I didn't see anyone like that.

The crowd was growing as more and more people were coming into the square. Men were wearing long jackets, tight pants, and shoes with big buttons on the toes. It was hard to tell who was balding and who wasn't since some men wore wigs. Most had hats on.

The women all wore long dresses. They carried parasols to shade themselves from the sun.

Everyone looked so formal. My jeans were new and had a neat sparkly design on them, but I still felt like I wasn't fancy enough to fit in.

I flipped to a blank page in my notebook and went up to a woman standing nearby. She was looking up at the balcony of Independence Hall.

"What are you watching for?" I asked, noticing that everyone around us was staring up at the same balcony.

"I am simply waiting," she replied, moving her parasol slightly to share her shade with me. The shade felt great. What a nice woman! "The Second Continental Congress has gathered inside the State House," she told me. Waving her arm around at the crowd, she said, "We are all waiting for word that the Declaration of Independence has been signed."

I wrote down the words "State House," then asked the woman where that was.

The woman looked at me as if I were crazy and

pointed at Independence Hall. I suddenly understood. I wrote down that in 1776, Independence Hall was called the State House.

If the Second Continental Congress was meeting right now, that meant Ben Franklin should be inside the State House with them. I wanted to be certain, so I asked, "Have you seen Benjamin Franklin today? It is very important that we find him."

Bo, Jacob, and Zack gathered around to hear the woman's reply.

"I have never heard the name you speak," she said with a small shake of her head. "Is Mr. Franklin from Philadelphia?"

I didn't know the answer.

Bo said softly, "No. He's from Boston, but he lives here now." She had to lean in to hear Bo speak. Bo spoke a tiny bit louder when he added, "Ben Franklin is definitely signing the Declaration of Independence today. He's one of nine people representing the State of Pennsylvania."

The woman thought about Bo's words, then said,

"I truly wish I could help you. I know the names of all fifty-six people signing the Declaration. But I have never heard of a Mr. Benjamin Franklin."

I thanked her and started to close my notebook. This was going to be harder than I expected. Drat that Babs Magee. What had she done to Ben Franklin?

Before I shut the notebook entirely, I turned back to the woman. "What's your name?" I asked, telling her I'd like to be able to remember her. She was very kind.

"Deborah Read," she replied, then pulled back her parasol and moved forward into the crowd, away from us.

Bo looked pale.

"What's up?" I asked.

"What's up?" Jacob and Zack echoed me.

Bo could barely speak. "This is terrible," he choked out.

"What?!" Jacob, Zack, and I shouted at the same time.

Bo took a few shallow breaths and stammered,

"That woman . . . Deborah Read . . . she is Ben Franklin's wife."

"I think we should say, Deborah Read *was* Ben Franklin's wife," Zack corrected. "We're stuck in a new version of American history. The world according to Babs Magee."

One thing was painfully clear: We had to find Ben Franklin. He had to sign the Declaration of Independence or else Babs would do it for him. There was no time to waste.

I crossed my fingers that we'd find him in time. Then, we all started running toward the entrance to State Hall.

CHAPTER FOUR

The Declaration of Independence

NO ONE STOPPED US AS WE RUSHED INSIDE AND HURried up the stairs.

"Over here." Jacob grabbed my arm and led us into a room full of men.

It looked like a schoolroom. Many men sat at small desks that were lined up in rows facing a long table. I almost expected to find Mr. C at the front.

Bo's head was rapidly flipping back and forth, practically spinning around on his neck.

"There"—he pointed at a man with long hair tied back in a bow—"that's John Hancock. He's the president of the Second Continental Congress. The struggle for America's freedom never would have happened without him." He cupped his hand over his mouth and whispered, "The British are offering a reward for his capture."

Bo's head spun the other direction. "And that man"—he tipped his head toward a man with curly red hair wearing a long black jacket—"that's Thomas Jefferson. He wrote the Declaration of Independence."

I double-checked the notes I'd taken earlier. "I thought you said five men created the Declaration." I took a long look at Thomas Jefferson.

"Five men were on the small committee, but Thomas Jefferson wrote the document by himself. Then Ben Franklin, John Adams, Roger Sherman, and Robert R. Livingston reviewed the work and made some changes." Bo led us a tiny bit closer to Thomas Jefferson. "I wish I wasn't so shy," Bo admitted. "I'd really like to meet Thomas Jefferson."

The meeting hadn't been called to order, yet. There was so much excitement. I could tell that these men didn't see each other very often. There were lots of handshaking and hugging going on. No one seemed to notice us even though we had wandered smack in the middle of the room.

"Go on. Talk to him," Zack encouraged. "Now's your chance."

Bo took one step closer to Thomas Jefferson and froze. "I can't do it." Bo stared down at his feet. "I don't know what I'd say."

Sometimes I can be bold for Bo and say stuff he's too shy to say, but this was something he'd have to do for himself. "It's okay, Bo," I said gently. "Maybe someday we can use the time-travel machine to visit Thomas Jefferson. I bet if the room weren't so crowded, you'd feel more brave."

Bo raised his eyes to mine. "I bet you're right," he said with a small smile. "I hope we can visit him soon."

I heard the word "slavery" brought up by two men behind us and asked Bo what they were talking about.

He glanced at Thomas Jefferson and said, "Thomas Jefferson had put in a paragraph against trading slaves, but not everyone agreed. It was a sticking point. The Declaration was almost not signed because of what he'd written."

I was shocked that anyone would disagree with Thomas Jefferson, especially on something as important as slavery, but Bo explained, "In 1776, slavery was an important issue, but not as important as declaring independence and starting our own country. In the end, the men of the Continental Congress decided that they would talk about slavery another time. For now, they would take out that paragraph and then sign the Declaration of Independence."

Bo told us that the document was changed and revised more than fifty times before this signing day arrived.

I tried to imagine what it must have felt like for Thomas Jefferson to scratch out part of the Declaration of Independence. It must have made him sad, and yet he had no choice if he wanted the entire Continental Congress to sign the document. I realized that the Declaration of Independence was just the beginning for this new country. There were a lot of things still to be decided. Even in our time, America was still changing.

Jacob pulled out the computer and took a peek at the screen. "We only have an hour and forty-one minutes left," Jacob reported. "Where is Ben Franklin?"

I scanned the room, searching for him. I let my eyes linger on each and every face. We couldn't convince Ben Franklin to sign the Declaration if we couldn't find him.

In the pit of my stomach, I felt that Babs was lurking somewhere. If Ben didn't sign the Declaration of Independence, she would. There were no girls in the room at all, except me. And no one wearing a yellow hat and coat. I wondered if she was wearing a disguise. . . .

BAM! With an echoing thump, John Hancock slammed a gavel on the small table. He sat in a plush chair and waited while the men in the room settled down. Thomas Jefferson handed him a piece of cream-colored parchment. The words on it were written by hand.

John Hancock began to read. "We hold these truths to be self-evident, that all men are created equal, that they are endowed by their Creator with certain unalienable Rights, that among these are Life, Liberty and the pursuit of Happiness."

We knew our time was ticking away, but not one of us could move. We were frozen to the floor. This was it! The signing of the Declaration of Independence.

When John Hancock finished reading, he took a feathered pen and signed his name in the middle of the page, right under the text, in a large, sweeping movement. He announced that representatives from each state would sign the document next. "There are some who are not with us today in Philadelphia," John Hancock informed us. "The document will be sent to them for their signatures," he concluded.

The pen was passed. Representatives from each state rose and went to the table to sign their names. We were waiting for Pennsylvania. Either Ben Franklin was going to suddenly show up or someone else was going to take his place. Someone sneaky, wearing a yellow coat.

I glanced around the room. No sign of Babs yet, but our history books clearly said she signed the document. Could she be one of the people they would send the parchment to another day? I hoped not.

Georgia. North Carolina. South Carolina. Massachusetts. Men got up and signed under each colony's name.

Maryland. Virginia. And then . . . after half the colonies had signed, John Hancock announced, "Pennsylvania."

Eight men rose and approached the table. Bo had said Ben was one of nine.

The first man took up the quill pen and dipped it in the ink. Done, he passed the pen to another. Where was the ninth person? Babs was here somewhere. I was sure of it. But where? Where??

Just as that man set the pen back on the table, a loud cheer came up from the crowd outside. Bo, Jacob, Zack, and I turned toward the balcony to see what had happened.

It was nothing important. Someone below was reporting to the crowd the names of the representatives who had already signed.

By the time we turned our attention back to the small table, Babs Magee was setting down the pen.

"You're too late," Babs said to us with a grin. "You missed me coming in the back door. I've already signed my name." Her yellow coat and matching hat looked completely out of place in the room full of men dressed in black.

Mr. Caruthers had said we might face danger when we ran into Babs. Zack hates danger. So I was doubly surprised to see him lunging at her. "Where's Ben Franklin?" Zack shouted as he bumped Thomas Jefferson to the ground in his attempt to get at Babs.

Zack had her by the legs, but Babs didn't seem to care. She didn't even fight him off.

"He's not here," she answered, quite pleased with herself. "Has anyone here seen Benjamin Franklin?" she called out to the gathering.

There was a lot of muttering, but no one had even

heard of him. Apparently, Babs had been living Ben Franklin's life for a while already.

"Release Miss Magee, at once!" one of the men in the Philadelphia delegation called out.

Zack let go of her legs and slid to the floor in defeat.

There was no danger here. Babs had already signed the Declaration. There was nothing more we could do. Even if we found Ben Franklin, we couldn't erase what she'd done.

"Ben Franklin is gone from American history," Babs said, smiling broadly from ear to ear. "I just signed the Declaration of Independence." She pointed at the time-travel computer in Jacob's pocket. "Go home and read all about it in your history books, kids!" And with that, she sat down at one of the desks reserved for the members of the Second Continental Congress.

Jacob helped Zack up.

I noticed that Thomas Jefferson was still sprawled out on the floor, right where Zack had accidentally shoved him. John Hancock rose from his chair and was headed purposefully across the room toward Thomas Jefferson, asking him if he was injured.

"None the worse for wear," Thomas Jefferson replied as he sat up.

I gave Bo an encouraging nudge in the back.

Bo knew that now was his chance to help his hero. He straightened his backbone, puffed out his chest, and stepped forward, hand outstretched. Thomas Jefferson took Bo's hand and pulled himself off the floor. "Thank you, son," he said to Bo.

Bo didn't reply. He just stared down at his hand. He was still gripping Thomas Jefferson's fingers. I had to give Bo a little reminder to drop Thomas Jefferson's hand. "Time to go," I whispered.

Bo let go of the future third president of the United States and said softly, "You're welcome."

Once we were in the courtyard below, I smacked myself on the forehead. "What are we going to do now?"

"How are we ever going to find Ben Franklin?" Zack half-grunted, half-sighed.

Jacob suggested that we move to a quiet corner

where no one could see us. Behind the State House, he said, "We need to find the exact moment Babs took over Ben Franklin's life."

Bo was still dazed from talking to Thomas Jefferson. He shook his head to clear it and added, "Mr. C said to use my knowledge. So"—he paused to rub his chin—"we can time-travel forward to the signing of the United States Constitution. If Babs Magee was here, she'll definitely be there, too. But if we want to catch her before she changes history, I think it makes more sense to go backward. Maybe we should go to the day he did his famous kite experiment."

"I vote for the kite experiment," Zack suggested.

"Me too," I said, and when Bo agreed, I turned to Jacob. "Can you get us there?"

He already had Mr. C's small screwdriver in his hand. "I'm willing to try."

"June sixteenth, 1752," Bo told him.

Jacob took the cartridge out of the computer. Our green glowing time-travel hole opened in the ground nearby.

"Don't get too close," Jacob warned us. "That hole

will take us straight back to school. It isn't the hole we need."

Jacob quickly unscrewed the back panel of the cartridge, just like Mr. C had told him. He peered inside and studied the wires for a long second. Then, he disconnected a wire and put the cartridge back together again.

I braced myself for an explosion. Just in case. But there was nothing.

"Whew," Zack said, relieved. "We're still alive." Then he muttered under his breath, "So far."

When Jacob put the cartridge back in the computer, the green smoke turned pink.

"Jacob, you made it pink!" Zack exclaimed, carefully looking at the time-travel hole. "What did you do to the green smoke?"

Jacob tapped his foot as he reviewed what he'd done. "I'm positive I disconnected the right wire," he said. Then, after a pause, he added, "Well, I'm almost sure."

Zack took a step back. "I have enough concerns about jumping into a green glowing hole. There's no way I'm going to be the first one to leap into a pretty pink fluffy one."

I took one last look at the Liberty Bell and suddenly felt very brave. "I'll go first," I said. I held my breath and jumped into the hole.

One by one, the boys followed me farther back through time.

CHAPTER FIVE

1752

It was dark, even though it was daytime. Black clouds surrounded the sun. And it was cold. Wind was blowing my hair into my eyes. I wrapped my arms around myself and shivered.

"It looks like it's gonna rain," Zack said, just before the clap of thunder boomed across the sky.

"You're a genius," Jacob told his brother. By his tone, I could tell he didn't really mean it. It was totally obvious that it was about to rain. A gust of wind whipped through me as another crash of thunder echoed all around.

"I *am* a genius," Zack responded. "You just don't accept that I am the smarter twin."

“Ha-ha,” Jacob snorted as he moved toward Zack with a threatening look on his face.

It was Bo’s day to keep Jacob and Zack from fighting. Once again, he stepped between them. “Ben Franklin should be around here somewhere,” Bo said, then asked Jacob to check the date. It was June 16, 1752.

“Great.” Bo motioned to an open field in front of us. “No one knows the exact date for sure, but many historians believe that today’s the day Ben Franklin is doing his most famous experiment. He’s going to prove that lightning is a natural form of electricity.”

“I thought Ben Franklin invented electricity,” I said, pulling out my notebook and pencil.

“Lots of people think that,” Bo told me. Bo explained that ideas about electricity had been around for a long time. By 1752, Ben Franklin had already studied electric sparks and electric shocks before he decided to check out lightning.

A big gust of wind blew, and I slammed the cover of my notebook shut. I didn’t want the pages to get wet.

Lightning flashed across the sky. I counted the

seconds between the lightning and the sound of its thunder. "One Mississippi. Two Mississippi. Three—" BOOM!

"That lightning was close to us," I told the boys.

"Too close," Zack said. "Dad told us that it's dangerous to be in an open field when there's lightning." He pointed to a small wooden shack a short distance away. "Let's go there," he suggested.

When another flash of lightning shot through the clouds, followed almost immediately by thunder, he didn't need to convince us. We took off running toward the shack.

It was empty. And small. Almost too small to fit all four of us. I didn't even think the wood building could be called a shack. It only had three walls and a roof. One side was entirely open. And through that side, we could see it had begun to rain.

"Awesome!" Bo suddenly exclaimed. "Look what I found." Bo was standing in the back of the shack. In his hand, he was holding a kite.

I moved closer to Bo, away from the open side of the shack, and flipped my notebook to a blank page.

I made a little sketch of the kite Bo was holding.

"Is that Ben Franklin's kite?" I asked, leaning in for a closer look.

"I think so. Once I read a description of it." Bo paused to rub his chin and gather his thoughts before continuing. "The kite was made of two crossed cedar strips." Bo pointed to the two flat wooden sticks. "A large, silk handkerchief." He showed us the diamond-shaped fabric of the kite. "It had a sharp pointed wire on top to attract the lightning." There was the wire.

"And," Bo went on, "Ben Franklin's kite had a key tied at the end of a long silk string. If the experiment was successful, when the kite was hit by lightning, the key would give off small shocks of electricity—"

I saw the dangling key before Bo pointed to it.

"This is Ben Franklin's kite!" I cheered. My happy moment only lasted a second. "But where is Ben Franklin?"

Bo looked down at the kite in his hand and shrugged.

Now, it was pouring hard. Even though we were standing in the shelter, we were still getting wet from the windswept rain.

Jacob checked the computer. "There's one hour and one minute left." He tucked the computer under his shirt to keep it dry.

Bo suggested we hang out for a minute or so. Maybe Ben Franklin was running late.

I crossed my fingers that today was the right day and that he'd show up. I started to count to sixty.

We had stood in silence for twenty-two seconds when Zack decided he'd entertain us. "What did the lightning bolt say to the other lightning bolt?" he asked.

Jacob wasn't going to play. Neither was Bo. They turned away to check out the kite and talk about how it was made. Something about how important it was that the string was made of silk. And that the string didn't get wet.

I yawned at them and said to Zack, "I give up. What did one lightning bolt say to the other?"

"You're shocking!" Zack laughed so hard, he

stumbled backward. "Want to hear another one?" he asked as he steadied himself.

"Sure," I said. The minute was almost up, but there was no sign of Ben Franklin. If he didn't show up, I wasn't sure what we'd do next.

"What's worse than raining buckets?" Zack asked.

I said I didn't know.

"Hailing taxis," Babs Magee answered the joke as she stepped into the shelter. There was water dripping off the brim of her yellow hat.

"What are *you* doing here!?" I yelled, startled by her sudden appearance. "And what have you done with Ben Franklin!?"

Babs didn't answer. She snagged the kite, string and all, out of Bo's hand. "Ben Franklin isn't coming today," she replied casually as she straightened the string.

"What do you mean he's not coming?" Zack demanded to know. I could see that Zack was about to pounce on her again. I put my hand out to stop him.

As mad as I was to see her, it wouldn't do us any good to attack her. She might time-travel away and we'd never have a chance to find Ben.

Maybe, if I asked the right question, she'd accidentally give a clue to where we could find him. I always had a lot of questions . . . all I needed was one really good one.

"Why isn't he coming?" I asked. This was the best question I could think of.

"You're too late!" Babs echoed the words she'd said at the signing of the Declaration of Independence. And with that, she tossed the kite up and out of the shelter.

The wind caught the kite and carried it up and up.

Babs was careful to keep her body under the shelter of the shack with us, keeping the bottom part of the string dry.

Bo leaned over and said quietly, "If the string in her hand gets wet, when the lightning hits the metal wire, electricity will travel past the key and Babs will be zapped."

"Hmm," I replied. As horrible as it sounds, I have to admit, I considered the possibility. No Babs. No more trouble with history.

Too bad we were such good kids.

No, we couldn't hurt her. In fact, we needed to trick her into giving us a clue to find Ben Franklin.

It was then I realized that Babs *had* given us a clue. She'd said, "You're too late."

And she was right, 1752 was simply too late. We were at the wrong moment in Ben Franklin's life. Babs must have knocked him off track before today. We had to pop backward again.

"Forget about Babs," I said, and told the boys that we should get going. "There's nothing more we can do here," I whispered so Babs wouldn't hear. "We have to go to an earlier point in Ben's life and hope to find—"

I was interrupted by a clap of thunder tied with a flash of lightning. They happened together. At the exact same moment. The lightning had struck right above our heads.

The key! Suddenly the key tied to the kite started buzzing. Humming. And shooting off small sparks of light. Like mini bolts of lightning.

"I did it!" Babs cried out. "Another feather in

my famous cap." She carefully held up the string with the key dangling in front of her. "Who wants to share my glory?" she asked, turning slightly to hold the key right in front of Jacob. "Go ahead," she teased him. "Put your knuckles against the key. You'll feel a light shock, proving once and for all that lightning is electric!"

I could see Jacob's fist trembling. He wanted to touch it. He really did.

"You can't do it, Jacob," Zack pleaded with his twin. "It's Ben Franklin's experiment. If you touch it, it'll be like it's okay that Babs took over."

"You don't understand." Jacob's hand crept a bit closer to the key. "This experiment led Ben Franklin to make up many words we still use today when we talk about electricity. Words like: battery, minus, plus, charged, conductor, condenser . . ." His knuckles were right next to the buzzing key.

"The thing is," Jacob went on, "this experiment in electricity, more than any other, was the beginning of all the scientific discoveries leading up to that thing I love the best—the first computer!"

Now I understood why Jacob wanted to touch the key so badly. If he touched the key, he'd be touching history.

"Please, Jacob," Zack began. "Don't touch it. Ben Franklin should be holding the key, not Babs Magee." Even when he was seriously begging, Zack could rhyme.

With a heartfelt groan and a huge sigh, Jacob let his hand drop. "You're right," he told his brother. "Maybe you are a genius after all." He stopped for a second, then added, "Nah. Just kidding." Jacob laughed. Instead of touching the key, he used his knuckles to give Zack a noogy on his head.

Babs snatched the key toward herself, muttering, "More fame for me."

Jacob was clearly disgusted with Babs. In a lightning-fast move, he whipped out our time-travel computer and asked Bo privately where we should go next.

Bo told him we should go to 1751 to see the first public hospital. Jacob pulled out the cartridge and the green time-travel hole opened in the back of the shed. Quickly, Jacob opened the cartridge, tweaked

the wires, and slammed the cartridge back into the computer. The green hole changed to a glowing dark blue.

The boys eagerly jumped in. Even Zack.

I hesitated. Babs was standing with the kite, touching the key with her closed fist, feeling the little electric shocks, rejoicing in her stolen discovery.

I couldn't help it. Really. My arms acted entirely on their own.

I took a quick step forward and shoved her. Hard. Babs fell back into the pouring rain. She stumbled. Babs Magee landed with a splash in a very large mud puddle. Her kite broke in half. The key buzzed its last electric buzz.

"That's for Benjamin Franklin," I shouted. "Wherever he is!" And with that, I jumped into the time-travel hole.

CHAPTER SIX

Searching

THERE'S SO MUCH THAT HAPPENED NEXT.

We were jumping in and out of history at the speed of light. One minute here. Two minutes there. Since the kite experiment in 1752, we'd been to 1751 and witnessed Babs Magee design the first public hospital. Instead of medical care being only for the rich who could afford it, this hospital was for everyone. One more good idea stolen from Ben Franklin.

From there we went to 1750 and saw Babs Magee invent the lightning rod, another of Ben's famous experiments involving electricity and lightning. Babs hoisted a long rod to the roof of her Philadelphia home. A crowd had gathered to see what she'd created.

Babs told everyone, including Jacob, Zack, Bo, and me, that the rod was made of iron. It attracted lightning and, when struck, the electric charge would travel directly to the ground and fizzle out instead of hit the roof and start a big fire.

The crowd cheered for Babs's invention, and we left 1750 feeling totally bummed.

In 1741 Babs invented a stove called the Pennsylvania Fire-Place. Old stoves did nothing to heat the room. Most of the warmth from a small fire escaped up the chimney. The Pennsylvania Fire-Place solved that problem, making the room nice and toasty. This new invention immediately became a bestseller, especially during the winter, when Philadelphia was freezing cold and covered with snow.

When Babs first lit a fire in the new stove, I hoped the whole thing would blow up in her face, but it turned out that Babs had studied history and knew not just *when* but *how* things were done. The stove worked perfectly.

Bo told us that the invention should have been called the "Franklin Stove," but the people we heard out on the street were cheering the greatness of the "Magee Stove." At that, Zack complained he was going to throw up.

After we saw Babs become the first postmaster of Philadelphia, set up the first fire department, and establish the first public library, we finally stopped for a short break. Time travel can make you really tired.

Besides, there were only forty-six minutes left on the computer and we needed to ask Bo where to go next.

It was 1729. Babs was about to buy the *Pennsylvania Gazette* newspaper, just like Ben Franklin had done. We were across the street from a small print shop. The sign said: MAGEE PRINTING OFFICE.

Babs was standing outside the office, entertaining people of the town and telling them about her grand plans for the paper. She was talking so loudly, we could hear every word. We tried to block out her voice while we talked.

"I'm starting to think we might never find Ben Franklin," Zack commented as he plopped down on a patch of grass and put his head in his hands. "How can I convince him to get back on track like Mr. C said if we can't find him? We don't even know what track it is that he needs to get back on." Zack huffed a bunch of short sighs. "At this rate, when we finally do find him, he'll be a baby."

I lay down on the grass next to Zack. I was feeling bad too. We weren't getting any closer to finding Ben Franklin. "The problem is," I said, "Ben Franklin did too many great things."

"Babs is taking over all of them," Jacob added, coming to sit with us.

Bo was still standing. He rubbed his chin. "I've led us all over Philadelphia, through forty-seven years of his inventions, discoveries, and political works." His shoulders drooped as he grumbled, "I'm running out of ideas."

We were all feeling sad. It didn't help that Babs was so nearby, going on and on about the new printing press she'd just bought from England. Something about the way she was moving her arms reminded me of the picture in our textbook.

In the sketch, Babs was a printer. She was showing

other people how the printing press worked.

I reached into my pocket and rubbed my fingers over the smooth cover of my little notebook. A question immediately came to me.

I pulled out the notebook and asked Bo, "Of all the things Ben Franklin did in his life, why would the makers of our social studies textbook choose a picture of him being a printer? Why isn't the drawing of Ben Franklin signing the Declaration of Independence instead? Or flying a kite?"

"Or starting a newspaper?" Zack put in, causing us all to glance across the street at Babs Magee.

Bo rubbed his chin and said, "Being a printer led to everything else Ben Franklin did during his life." And as he said it, Bo's eyes grew wide. "That's it!" he exclaimed. "Because Ben Franklin was a printer, he was able to write all his political ideas in his own newspaper. He made cartoons expressing his opinions. Selling papers made him wealthy. He used his money to pay for his inventions."

I quickly jumped up. "Bo," I asked, "when did Ben Franklin first become a printer?"

Bo looked over at the print shop for the *Pennsylvania Gazette.* "I'd have guessed it was officially today," he said as he squinted his eyes at Babs Magee. She was still bragging about the newspaper to anyone who'd listen.

Jacob suggested we ask around to see if anyone in 1729 had heard of Ben Franklin.

There was a store nearby. It had a big sign on the door: SMITH'S DRY GOODS. A tall, thin man was standing behind the counter, writing down a woman's purchases in a small receipt book. He was wearing a beige apron.

Even though I knew our time was running out, I didn't want to interrupt. We waited patiently behind her. When it was our turn, the man asked what we wanted to buy.

"Nothing," I admitted. "We're looking for Ben Franklin."

The man seemed disappointed that we weren't buying anything. "Never met him," he answered coolly.

Jacob got all excited. "But you've heard of him?" he asked, the words coming out in a rush.

"Sure," the man said. "Everyone has heard of Ben Franklin. He is famous."

"Famous for printing the *Pennsylvania Gazette*?" I wondered.

The man wrinkled his nose at me. "Where are you from? The people of Philadelphia all know that Miss Magee now owns the newspaper." The man wiped his hands on his apron and came around the counter. He picked up a thick, round candle off a nearby shelf.

"These are the best quality candles in all thirteen colonies." He flipped the candle over so I could see the underside. "They come directly from the candle shop in Boston."

"Uh-oh," I said as I took the candle from him and quickly passed it to Bo, who handed it to Jacob and then to Zack.

There on the bottom of the candle was the candle maker's label: B. FRANKLIN. BOSTON, MASSACHUSETTS.

"Do you want to buy the candle or not?" the man asked me.

"No thanks." We didn't have any money anyway.

I was sweating when I set the candle back on the shelf. We all hurried outside the dry goods shop.

Babs Magee was still standing outside her printing office. I caught her eye. She winked at me. I knew what that wink meant. We were too late again.

Drat. Double drat.

CHAPTER SEVEN

Boston

WITH THIRTY-TWO MINUTES LEFT ON OUR CARTRIDGE, and the fear of failure looming over us, we knew we had to leave Philadelphia. Since we now knew that Ben Franklin was a candle maker in 1729, I thought we should stay in 1729 and look for him at his candle factory in Boston. Bo was pretty sure that if we wanted to catch him before Babs took over, we'd need to go back further. He agreed that we should go to Boston, but in 1718 instead. Bo hadn't steered us wrong yet, so we decided to try.

We landed in a main shopping area. The weather was nice and the street was busy. There were people walking around with packages, popping in and out of stores.

Over the shops were little signs. One had a picture of a knife on it. Another had a pair of scissors. A brass pot hung over one door.

"Cutler, haberdasher, and brazier," Bo explained, following my eyes as they stopped on each sign. "A cutler makes, sharpens, and repairs knives. A haberdasher is like a tailor. A brazier makes and repairs brass objects."

"What's that one?" I asked him, pointing to a shop across the street. There was a different sign over that door. There were no words, just a brightly painted blue ball.

"That's the one we're looking for," Bo said, studying the sign. "A blue ball hung outside the Franklin family candle shop."

Jacob gave Bo an encouraging slap on the back. "You've done great today. We couldn't have gotten this far without you. Let's hope Ben's here, so we can start undoing the damage Babs Magee did to American history."

We all agreed to be very cautious and keep an eye out for Babs.

We scanned the street. She wasn't there, so we went into the candle shop.

"Pe-ew," I blurted, the instant we stepped inside. The candle shop smelled disgusting, kind of like burned steak. I plugged my nose. Jacob and Bo were fanning themselves. Zack had pulled up the collar of his T-shirt and was breathing through the fabric.

Bo quickly explained that candles in 1718 were made of animal fat called tallow. Tallow smelled bad. We each took a few small breaths to get used to the smell.

Colored candles were hanging on ropes along the walls. There was a long worktable, kind of like Mr. C's workbench, down the center of the room. A stove at one side had pots sitting nearby. And in the back of the room were a lot of big, round, wooden shipping barrels.

Sitting in the corner of the shop was a boy. He looked like he was only a few years older than we were. He was reading a book.

Because there was a bell tied to the shop door, the

boy raised his head when we entered, but quickly lowered it again. He ignored us.

The boy was wearing a clean suit with knee-length pants. His blondish-brown hair was long and hung in his eyes. His white socks were pulled way up. A work apron was tied over his outfit.

I boldly went up to him first. "Hi," I said cheerfully. "We're searching for Ben Franklin. Have you seen him?"

The boy didn't glance up at me, but continued to read while he talked. "I am Polly Baker," he said quickly. "Never heard of Ben Franklin."

Zack raised his eyebrows and said to the boy, "Are you serious? Your name can't really be Polly. That's a girl's name."

Keeping his eyes pinned to the page in front of him, the boy laughed, his smile reaching ear to ear. "Did I say Polly? My name is actually Silence Dogood."

Zack leaned over and whispered to me, "That's not any better. If silence was a name, I think it would be for a girl."

"Silence," I said, trying not to giggle at the boy's name. I reminded myself that there were a lot of weird names in the olden days. "Have you seen Ben Franklin? We have to find him. It's an emergency."

"In truth, I am not Silence Dogood. My name is Richard Saunders."

At least that was a boy's name.

Bo suddenly started laughing. "Polly! Silence! Richard! Ben Franklin used all three of those names during his lifetime. He liked to write under different names to hide his identity. They call those 'pseudonyms.' "

"Are you saying this guy"—I pointed to the boy—"is really Ben Franklin?" I asked Bo.

Bo nodded. He was grinning.

It was so exciting! We'd finally found him. But Ben Franklin clearly didn't want to be found. He went back to reading his book.

I pulled out my notebook. "Why's Ben working here?" I asked Bo after finding a clean page. "Shouldn't he be at school?"

Bo rubbed his chin and said, "I remember reading

that Ben Franklin only went to school for two years. When he was ten, his dad couldn't afford to send him anymore. So Ben came home and started working in the candle shop. That was two years ago."

"Makes me feel pretty lucky to be in school," Jacob remarked. "I don't want to be working yet."

"And I haven't decided what to be when I grow up," Zack added.

"Neither has Ben Franklin," Bo put in. "He was twelve when he first became a printer."

"How old is he now?" I asked.

"Twelve," Bo answered.

"Then this must be the moment when Babs knocked Ben Franklin off his life's course," I said happily. "Now, all we have to do is convince him to be a printer instead of a candle maker."

"It's my turn at last," Zack said, taking an eager step forward. He began to tell Ben Franklin that we'd come from the future. How he was missing from our textbooks. That Babs Magee had stolen his place in history.

"Time travel?" Ben Franklin snorted, putting down

his book. "Ha!" He began to laugh. "Next thing I know, you'll tell me the colonies are no longer controlled by the British." He held his belly as he laughed harder. "You"—he pointed to Zack—"are a jokester."

Zack gave me a sideways glance and muttered, "When I try to be funny, no one laughs. Now, when I'm serious, Ben Franklin is going to wet his pants."

Ben Franklin didn't stop laughing until the bells on the shop door chimed. Then, he quickly grabbed his book and ducked behind the row of round, wooden barrels near the back of the shop. Ben Franklin was the fastest ducker I've ever seen.

A man had come into the store. He was wearing a suit and carrying a walking stick. "Have you seen Ben?" he asked politely.

Zack was about to point to the barrels, when Jacob said suddenly, "He stepped out to run an errand." Then, Jacob mouthed to us, "Ben Franklin doesn't have time to help customers. Zack needs more time to convince him."

Loudly to the man, Jacob added, "He'll be back soon."

"Fine and well," the man told Jacob. "I am pleased to hear that he is out on shop business. I shall return later." The door chime rang as the man left.

"My brother James," I heard Ben say with a sigh from behind the barrels. "He recently opened his own print shop nearby. When he has a few minutes to spare, he humors himself by checking on me to see if I am working. Or not."

"How many siblings do you have?" I called out to Ben from behind the barrels.

"Fifteen," came his muffled reply.

I have one older sister. Jacob and Zack have a younger brother. Bo's an only child. Sixteen kids is a whole mess of kids. In our time, the Franklin family would need a school bus just to get around town.

In the next few minutes, we chased away two more customers.

"Why is this shop so busy?" Zack groaned. "I'm never going to get a chance to convince Ben."

Bo explained that before electricity, candles were

super important. "You needed candles to see where you were going, to read at night, to have dinner—basically to see anything after dark."

I wrote down what Bo had said about candles. I also make a note that Ben had fifteen brothers and sisters and that we'd met one named James. I thought it might be important to remember that James was also a printer.

I asked Ben Franklin if he liked being a candle maker.

"No," he replied. "It's horrible. The shop smells terrible. The work is repetitive and boring. Plus, there's no time to read."

"I've got it!" Zack said suddenly, slapping himself on the forehead. "Now I know how to convince him to become a printer. We've gotta get him out of here."

Jacob rolled his eyes. "There isn't enough time, Zack. We only have half an hour left on the computer."

Zack pointed at Ben still hiding amongst the barrels. "Sometimes it's easier to find what you *want* to do by figuring out what you *don't* want to do. It's the same thing I do with the school clubs." Zack smiled. "We already know he hates making candles. Let's go show him some more horrible jobs! By the time we're done, he'll be begging to be a printer.

"Come on," Zack told Ben, taking him by the arm. "We're going for a quick spin around the block." When Ben protested, Bo helped by telling Zack that Ben was a health nut. Zack suggested he needed some fresh air and time away from the stinky tallow.

It worked. Ben agreed to come with us. We all went into the shop next door together. A man was leaning over a spinning stone sharpening knives.

"You said you hate making candles," Zack told Ben. "I think you should get out of there and try something else."

"I cannot," Ben groaned. "I will always be a chandler."

"You can always change your mind," Zack insisted as he pointed at the knife maker. "How about knives?" he encouraged Ben to try making one. The man in the shop agreed to give Ben a go at it.

Ben leaned over the stone and promptly sliced his finger. There was just a tiny drop of blood, but it was enough for Ben to say, "I don't want to make knives."

We left the shop.

The next building on the street was under construction. A man was laying bricks for a wall. Zack encouraged Ben to pick up a few bricks. Though Ben was strong, he put the bricks back down a second after he picked them up. "Dull work," he reported.

We hurried through the shops of a shoemaker, a tailor, and a barrel maker. None of the jobs were good for Ben Franklin. He told us that he really wanted to be a sailor, but his dad had said no. His dad wanted him to be a minister, but Ben had said no.

Zack was an expert at trying new things. In less than ten minutes, he'd helped Ben explore seven jobs. Ben didn't like any of them. As we walked back to the candle shop, Zack was telling Ben about all the great things he could do as a printer.

"You can read as much as you want, since you'll be printing the books. You can write articles—even under three different pseudonyms, if you want. Someday, you can even own a newspaper! Plus"—Zack winked at Bo—"with all the money you'll make, you can experiment and invent things."

"I've only created a few things so far. Like paddles used for swimming. But I have a number of great ideas." Ben stopped suddenly. "How do you know I want to invent things? I never told you that."

"Don't laugh," Zack said, "but we really did time-travel. I didn't know about the swim paddles. But in the future, you're going to invent a ton of useful stuff."

This time, Ben looked like he believed Zack. With a smile, Zack asked Ben, "What do you think, Polly? Wouldn't you like to be a printer?"

We'd returned to the Franklin family candle shop. Ben held the door open and we all went inside.

"Yes," Ben said thoughtfully as the door closed behind us. "I would like to be a printer."

"Hurray," Zack cheered. "My work here is done."

He took a little bow. "History is back on track. Let's go to school."

Jacob took the computer out of his pocket. With twenty minutes to spare, we'd done it. Ben Franklin wanted to be a printer. Then he'd live out the rest of his life just the way he was supposed to. And Babs Magee would disappear from our textbooks.

Jacob had his hand on the cartridge, ready to pull it out and take us home, when Ben Franklin sighed.

"One problem," he said as he picked up a candle mold and a container of hot tallow. "I cannot become a printer. It is simply not possible."

CHAPTER EIGHT

Too Late

THE DOOR CHIME RANG AGAIN. "BENJAMIN FRANKLIN," a familiar voice interrupted me from asking Ben why he couldn't be a printer. "I have come to see how you are doing in your new apprenticeship." It was a woman's voice, but whoever she was, she was standing in the shadows.

"Awful," Ben Franklin replied, setting the newly poured candle to cool near an open window. "I want to be a printer. Truly." Ben looked over at Zack with a horribly disappointed look on his face.

"Ah, too bad," the woman said, not really meaning it. When she stepped out of the darkness, there was no mistaking her yellow coat and matching hat.

"Babs Magee!" I exclaimed.

Jacob squinted his eyes at Babs and said in a low voice, "We will stop you from taking over Ben Franklin's life!"

"No, you won't. I'm unstoppable. As always, you're too late!" Babs's announcement echoed through the small shop. She reached into her coat pocket and pulled out . . . not her time-travel computer, as I'd hoped. If it had been, I'd have quickly made a grab for it. Snagging her computer would have been a perfect way to stop her from causing any more damage to American history. But she didn't take out her computer.

Out of her pocket, Babs pulled a rolled piece of parchment paper.

"This is a contract. It says that for the next nine years, Ben Franklin agrees to work here in the candle shop." Her eyes bounced from me to Bo to Jacob to Zack. "I convinced Ben to sign it today. If he breaks the contract, he'll go to jail.

"In 1718," Babs informed us, "children went to work. They became apprentices and learned about a business. When Ben Franklin was weighing his options, I suggested he talk to me because, as a stranger, I could offer him honest advice. I lied. Instead, I convinced him that he should work as a chandler in his father's shop. Ben's father was so grateful, he asked me to hold on to the contract for safekeeping."

"Are you kidding?" I said, moving in closer to see Ben's signature on the document.

"Ben is now an official apprentice to his father. He must study the craft of candle making and do whatever his father says." She waved the contract around. The paper made a crackling sound.

She glared at us with her beady eyes and teased, "See? Too late again!"

I would have panicked, but suddenly I figured out exactly why Ben's life was off track. I had to tell the boys.

While Babs was watching Ben Franklin make more candles, I gathered the boys in a corner. I whispered to Bo, "I bet that Ben Franklin was supposed to sign an apprentice agreement with his brother James instead of with his father. That way he'd have been a printer instead of a chandler."

By the look on Bo's face, I knew I was right. Babs had convinced Ben Franklin to sign the wrong apprentice document.

"Well, then, we have to find James. He's the only one who can help us now." I flipped back a few pages in my notes. James had been in the shop a short time earlier. I wondered where we could find him.

Jacob looked at the computer and reported, "We don't have much time left."

Just like Bo, I rubbed my chin while I reviewed my notes. Ben had said that James had recently opened his own print shop. "What if we hurry over to James's shop?" I asked Bo.

"It won't work." Zack wasn't just complaining this time. He was being realistic. "There's no guarantee we'd find him there. He might be out on an errand. We don't have enough time to run all over Boston looking for him."

It was starting to feel like all our hard work was for nothing. Babs was going to be in our history books. Forever.

My head was spinning with ideas. "Maybe if we

time-traveled again, we could visit James at night. He'd be asleep in bed. At least then, we'd be able to find him."

"That won't work either," Zack moaned. "James won't sign something if we wake him up. He'll think we're thieves and have us thrown into jail."

"That's it!" Bo called out.

"Huh?" Jacob, Zack, and I said at the same time.

"We have to go to jail," Bo said softly so Babs wouldn't hear him.

"What?!" Zack blurted out. His voice echoed loudly through the shop. Babs looked over at us.

"Trust me," Bo said. He whispered some instructions to Jacob. Our green hole opened in the floor while Jacob began using the screwdriver to take the back off the cartridge.

I ran across the room and, before Babs could stop me, I asked Ben Franklin if he wanted to time-travel. The inventor side of him was so curious, he immediately said he'd come—only if I promised to bring him back, of course. I swore I would. But I said it really softly so there was no way Babs knew we'd be coming back. I let her think we were taking Ben away forever.

I grabbed Ben's hand and we started running. The shop wasn't very big, and Jacob was still fiddling around with the wires in the cartridge. "Put on the brakes!" I shouted at Ben before he flew into the wrong hole. We didn't want to take him to school. We needed to keep him in the 1700s—only a different part of the 1700s.

Ben had no clue about brakes. But he knew enough to stop. We were teetering on the edge of the time-travel hole.

Babs was hustling across the shop after us. She was shouting that we had no right to takc Ben anywhere.

"You can't take him away from here! He has a duty to his father." Babs was coming at us, waving the candle apprentice contract. "As long as I have this contract, he's an apprentice. And I'm a printer!" She was so close, I could smell her breath. Ew. "You're too late!" she repeated.

I looked back and replied, "Maybe this time, you're too early."

"I'll find you," Babs said as she pulled her own time-travel computer out of her yellow coat pocket. "I'll follow you."

"Not if you don't know where we are going," Zack teased. "And I'm not telling." Very mature, Zack stuck his tongue out at her.

That just made Babs mad. She put her computer back in her pocket, saying, "If I can't follow you through my own time-travel hole, I'll just come with you in yours! I will stop you wherever you go. Ben Franklin's fame is my fame now."

She started coming toward our green hole, still grasping Ben's apprentice contract in her fist.

"Uh-oh," Jacob cried out. He was having trouble opening the little screws on the back of the cartridge. He wasn't going to be able to reset the wires and get the hole color changed in time.

Babs was coming on fast. "Hurry up," I begged Jacob to get a move on.

"I have an idea," Jacob said, bailing on the screwdriver. "But it's going to be messy."

"Just do it, Jacob." Zack took one look at Babs and shouted, "Whatever you have to do, do it!"

At his brother's encouragement, Jacob pocketed the small screwdriver. He ripped the top off the cartridge and yanked out a wire. He threw the wire on the floor.

Then Jacob slammed the top on the cartridge. An explosion rocked the room. I held tightly to Ben Franklin's hand, and together we fought the force of the blast. Through the explosion, I saw that the green hole had turned purple.

Ben and I inched our way to the glowing purple hole. Jacob, Zack, and Bo had already time-traveled. Ben and I toppled into the hole like Jack and Jill on a hill.

And Babs . . . the last thing I heard was her angry shout as the time-travel hole closed behind us, leaving her in 1718 all alone.

CHAPTER NINE

James Franklin

BEN FRANKLIN AND I LANDED IN A TANGLE OF ARMS and legs. We looked like a two-headed spider.

"We've got a problem," I told Jacob, who was standing the closest to us. Ben, slightly in shock, was trying to figure out which of the legs was attached to him.

Jacob immediately came to help. He moved my arm left and Ben's leg right. "There," he said as Ben and I were finally able to stand up. "Problem solved."

I was grateful for the help, but getting up wasn't the problem I was thinking of. "Babs still has the apprentice contract for Ben Franklin," I moaned. "We can't undo that contract and have Ben sign a new one until that one expires."

Jacob checked the computer. It read, TUESDAY, FEB. 12, 1723, and we only had eighteen minutes left.

"I wish," I began, "that there was still some way we could get that contract away from Babs."

"Hey, where is everyone?" It was Bo. He was over in a corner, a little ways from us. "Why's it so dark?"

I rushed over to Bo. He had a large piece of paper over his head. I whisked the paper away.

"Thanks," Bo said, rubbing his eyes. "I was worried I'd gone blind in the explosion."

"Maybe that's why Mr. C always gives us goggles," I replied. I started to crumple up the paper that had been on Bo's head, when his hand shot out and stopped me.

"Abigail, don't!" Bo snagged the paper from my hand. It was crumpled at the top where I'd begun to squish it. I'd thought it was trash.

Bo spread the paper out on his leg, wiping it with his hand to smooth the wrinkles I'd caused. "Sometimes wishes come true." He smiled broadly.

Ben and the twins came over to investigate. We all

saw that Bo was holding Ben Franklin's apprentice document!

I did a little victory dance. "Babs must have dropped it in the blast, and it fell through the hole before she could get it back! Yippee!" I wiggled my hips and spun around.

Bo ripped up Babs's contract, and then, the boys started dancing too. All the boys, I mean, except Ben Franklin.

"What's up?" Jacob asked him. "Now all we have to do is get James to take you on and you'll be a printer! American history will be back on track." He paused suddenly. "You do still want to be a printer, don't you?"

"Of course, I want to be a printer," Ben replied. "But signing the chandler agreement was important to my parents. I do not want to disappoint them."

Boy, I understood that. I wondered if Ben would get in trouble with his dad. I mean, as a chandler, he was helping in the family shop and all.

It was Zack who said, "I try a lot of things. I change my mind all the time. My dad just says that he wants me to be happy. I bet that if you told your dad that you'd rather be a printer, he'd be okay with it."

Ben looked a little scared to go to his father. He had his lips pinched together, and his eyebrows were raised. "All right," Ben said at last. "If James agrees to take me on as his apprentice, I will ask my father for permission."

Just then, I screamed. My voice echoed through the small room where we'd landed. "Eak!" I shrieked again, jumping up and down and pointing at a mouse that had stepped on my toe and was now slipping beneath an old desk. I wasn't scared. Just grossed out. Really.

Seeing the mouse reminded us where we were. Turns out, Bo had known that on February 12, 1723, James Franklin was in jail. Stuck in a cell, James would have to listen to us. There was nowhere he could go.

We left the room we'd landed in and ducked into the shadows of a long hallway.

Ben discovered which cell his brother was in. "James is over there," he said, and pointed.

There was only one British soldier guarding James's

cell. The man was sitting on a wooden chair, right in front of the cell door. We were going to have to cause a distraction.

"I have a plan," I said, and asked Ben to lend me his work apron. He handed it over, and I quickly ran back to where I'd seen the mouse. My furry little friend was scurrying along the wall, searching for food. I bent down and, careful not to touch him, I led the mouse onto Ben's apron and jiggled him into the pocket.

I hustled to where the boys were hiding. I could see the soldier. He was reading a newspaper.

Very softly and quickly, Bo told me the paper was the *New England Courant*. "That's James Franklin's newspaper. James is in jail for writing that he disagreed with the ideas of the church leaders. There wasn't freedom of the press, like in our time. The church leaders were mad and had him arrested. He'll be here for three months."

"What happens to the newspaper while James is in jail?" I whispered back. I could feel the mouse squirming to be set loose.

"According to history, his apprentice, Ben Franklin, will be in charge. If we don't succeed, I guess that—"

"Babs Magee will take over instead," Zack finished Bo's thought. I didn't even know Zack was listening to us. "Let's make sure it's Ben," Zack whispered.

I set Ben's apron on the ground and positioned the pocket toward the soldier. "Okay, Mickey," I said, giving my buddy a new name. "Let's hope this guard isn't as brave as he looks."

Feeling solid ground under his four little feet, the mouse began to scurry toward the soldier.

"Aughhhhh!" The soldier jumped off his chair and started screaming. He was swiping at Mickey with the rolled-up newspaper.

"Run, Mickey, run," I cheered softly. And he did. Mickey hustled down the hall with the soldier close on his heels. Mickey turned the corner, and so did the soldier. Now was our chance.

"Twelve minutes," Jacob notified us.

"James—" I started as I ran up to the cell.

Bo stopped me. "Abigail," he said. "It's Ben

Franklin's turn. He needs to get his life back on track. We can't do this part for him."

I stepped back away from the cell bars, and Ben stepped up.

They were whispering. I could barely hear what they were saying, and it was driving me crazy.

I did manage to catch James saying, "But I already have an apprentice."

Then more whispering, until Ben said, "I can run the paper while you are in jail. I will make deliveries. Sell newspapers on the corner. Clean the shop. I can write essays and draw cartoons."

James spoke a bit louder when he said, "I won't give you any money for your work."

And Ben replied in a clear voice, "I only need enough money to purchase food."

I leaned over to Bo. "Are you sure we're doing the right thing? It seems like a bad deal for Ben. Lots of work and no pay."

"That's the way Ben's apprenticeship worked," Bo replied. "Ben will learn a lot from his brother. But James will also be really mean to Ben while he works there. In a few years, Ben will get sick of it all and run away."

"We're convincing him to sign a document that he's going to break. Won't he go to jail?" I was worried.

"Not if he leaves Boston," Bo responded with a wink.

I understood. Ben would learn to be a printer, then he'd move to Philadelphia in order to escape working for his brother. We'd already seen all the great things that would happen once Ben Franklin moved to Philadelphia.

Ben and James had come to some kind of agreement. Ben turned away from the cell and said, "We need parchment and a quill in order to write the new contract."

I didn't have any parchment, but I had my small notebook.

Ben had never seen white paper with lines printed on it. Or a pencil. At first he looked a little afraid of them.

I was about to show him how the pencil worked, when Bo said, "Hang on." Bo rushed back to the first room and, when he returned, he had a piece of parchment and a quill pen. "I found these in that old desk. We can't have a historic document written in pencil," Bo explained.

Ben took the parchment and quill and scribbled out an agreement. Then, he rushed back to James's cell.

From down the hall, I heard the British solider calling, "Come back, you little varmint." I smiled, knowing Mickey would be just fine. He was a clever mouse.

Ben and James were still writing when Jacob pulled the cartridge out of the computer. The green hole opened in the hallway. Without feeling rushed, Jacob was able to concentrate on getting the back unscrewed. No more explosions. He attached two wires and closed the cartridge. Then the hole turned a lovely shade of orange.

We told Ben Franklin we had to go. It was time to take him home.

"Take me with you," James pleaded. "Do not leave me to rot in jail." I'm not sure if Ben had told him who we were. James just wanted out. He rattled the cell bars.

I was conflicted. No one should go to jail for speaking their beliefs. On the other hand, part of me wanted to tell him he deserved the stay in jail for the mean way he was going to treat Ben.

But what I thought didn't really matter. The fact was: Jail was an important part of James Franklin's history. Just like printing was part of Ben's.

We told James we were sorry we couldn't take him with us.

Jacob, Zack, Ben, Bo, and I all held hands and gathered around the pumpkin-colored time-travel hole.

On the count of three we jumped, and on four we landed, because time travel is really fast.

CHAPTER TEN

Home

WHEN WE GOT BACK TO BOSTON IN 1718, BABS WAS gone. Once she'd lost the apprentice agreement through the time-travel hole, she must have decided to give up and start preparing for her next victim instead. The bummer of it was that the way time travel worked, we'd have to wait until next Monday to find out what kind of trouble she was up to.

We were back in Ben's dad's candle shop. Jacob told us we only had three minutes left on the computer. Since James and Ben had made an apprentice agreement, we figured all we had to do was say good-bye.

Suddenly the door of the shop flew open. The man who entered stomped into the room, shouting, "Where have you been?"

"Well, we went to—" Zack began.

"Not you!" the man bellowed. He turned to face Ben Franklin. "Benjamin Franklin! Where have *you* been?" He didn't wait for an answer, though. He went on and on about how there had been customers and no one to help them. How the day's candles hadn't been poured. The tallow had gone cold.

Ben Franklin was still holding the new contract he'd agreed to with James. I hoped he was brave enough to tell his father about it.

In the future, Ben Franklin would do so many courageous things. Becoming James's apprentice was the first step to his fame.

Ben stared at his father for a long minute. Too long. Our computer started to beep.

Because it was so important that we jumped home before our two hours ran out, Mr. C had installed a warning buzzer. And now, as the tension in the room was so thick, we could barely breathe, the beeping had begun.

Ben Franklin cast a sideways glance at us.

"We have to go," Zack explained. "Our time is up."

Ben nodded. "Is American history back on track?" he asked.

"The history of the Unites States is up to you, now," Jacob told him, looking quickly from Ben to his dad and then back again.

There was curiosity in Ben's eyes when he asked, "What are these 'United States'?"

I smiled. "When you're a printer, you will write articles that will help turn the colonies into states. Later, someone else will come along to unite them." I thought about Abraham Lincoln and winked at the boys.

"Hmm," Ben Franklin said thoughtfully, then repeated the phrase "United States."

Ben's father was tapping his foot.

I would have liked to hear Ben Franklin tell his father that the apprentice document had been destroyed. And that he wanted to be a printer's apprentice to his brother instead. But there was no time.

The computer was beeping wildly. "One second," Jacob announced suddenly. He immediately pulled the cartridge out of the back. Our green time-travel hole opened in the floor nearby. And away we jumped.

In the end, we didn't even get a chance to say good-bye.

We landed in the school cafeteria.

We ran. Down the hall. Through the gym. Hopping down the stairs. Straight to Mr. C's laboratory under the school.

At the large wooden door, we knocked. Mr. C called, "Come in," and we did.

"Welcome back," Mr. C said as he tossed a black cloth over the project he'd been working on. It was a sphere. That was all we knew about his new invention.

"I was waiting for you," Mr. C said. "I've been so nervous, I could hardly work at all." He snatched up his textbook teacher's guide and set it out on the table. "This must have been a tough adventure," he said. "How did it go?"

"Well," I answered for us all, "to be honest, we aren't sure what happened in the end. We ran out of time."

"Let's check." Mr. C started flipping through the pages of his book, looking for Ben Franklin.

I was worried.

So was Zack. "What if," he began, "Ben Franklin simply quit his dreams and never became a printer? What if he remained a chandler? What if we light Franklin candles on my next birthday? What if—"

"Knock it off, Zack." Jacob got in Zack's face. "No use in freaking out before Mr. C checks his book."

Zack puffed out his chest, saying, "What if James changed his mind and—"

Bo wedged himself between the boys, ready to break up the fight. But, suddenly, Jacob and Zack were laughing.

"We tricked you!" Zack told Bo.

"It was Zack's idea," Jacob said, still giggling. "He knows you hate it when we argue."

Bo rolled his eyes. "Just wait," he warned. "I don't only read biographies. I've read a few books of tricks and jokes myself. When you least expect it—"

Bo didn't finish. Mr. C interrupted: "I found the page."

Slowly, we approached Mr. C's worktable.

In the middle of page 144 was a painting of Benjamin Franklin! In the picture, Ben was showing a printing press to two men.

"Whew," Mr. C said, wiping the back of his hand across his forehead. "That was close." He was very happy that we'd saved American history. Again.

"We did our best," Jacob said. "And we worked together as a team. Just like you told us to." Jacob gave Mr. C the computer and cartridge. He told our teacher how he'd had to tweak the wires. And even how we'd used the explosion to escape from Babs.

I gave Mr. C his notebook and pencil. I told him thinking like a detective had helped me figure out a bunch of things, like about being too late and how we needed James to apprentice Ben. Mr. C asked if he could read what I'd written. "Of course," I agreed.

"I'm going to try Pottery Club tomorrow," Zack announced. "Just one more thing I'd like to check out." Zack told Mr. C about how he helped Ben Franklin try a bunch of different jobs in 1718. "I'm

super glad I don't have to decide what I want to be when I grow up, yet," Zack added.

"And what did you do, Bo?" Mr. C asked, knowing Bo wouldn't share on his own.

Bo pointed at page 144. Under the picture was a time line. The time line showed all the great things Ben Franklin did during his lifetime. "That's what I did," Bo said proudly, albeit softly.

Mr. C closed his book with a smile.

As we walked out the laboratory door, I turned and asked, "Mr. C, on this adventure, Babs was jumping all over Ben Franklin's life. How are we going to find her next time?"

"Luck," was all he said. And he closed the door behind us.

A Letter to Our Readers

Dear Readers,

Ben Franklin's Fame is a mixture of fact and fiction. The fiction part is all the stuff we made up, like the kids, and the time travel, and Babs Magee.

But it is a fact that there really was a person named Ben Franklin. It is true that he was one of the greatest Americans who ever lived and that is why we wanted Jacob, Zack, Abigail, and Bo to go meet him.

It is also true that Ben Franklin worked for his father, Josiah. But he was never apprenticed as a chandler. Ben went to school for two years to become a minister, but when his father ran out of money, Ben came home. He wanted to be a sailor, but his parents didn't like that idea.

Josiah Franklin took twelve-year-old Ben all around Boston to see different kinds of jobs. Ben made knives for a while, then candles in his dad's shop. He also thought about becoming a shoemaker, a bricklayer, a barrel maker, and a tailor. There were so many things Ben was interested in.

But mostly, Ben Franklin loved to read. He'd spend all his money on books, then sell them to get new books. Working in a print shop allowed Ben to be around books, to write and read. He was apprenticed to his brother James for nine years. In 1723, while James was in jail, Ben ran the paper himself.

Right after James was released, Ben broke his apprenticeship contract and ran away. To avoid arrest, he snuck onto a boat and ended up sailing to Philadelphia.

Ben bought the *Pennsylvania Gazette* and opened his own print shop. From the shop he was an inventor, politician, soldier, statesman, poet, ambassador, shopkeeper, bookseller, printer, cartoonist, scientist, journalist, chess player, weight lifter, and still . . . a reader.

In this book, we told you about many of the inventions Ben Franklin made. But he was also one of the great politicians and thinkers for America when our country was first forming. He signed the Declaration of Independence. He made treaties with France and Great Britain. And he signed his name on the U.S. Constitution.

Ben Franklin was an amazing man. His contributions to America will never be forgotten.

Enjoy,

Stacia and Rhody

We hope you liked Blast to the Past: *Ben Franklin's Fame.* Watch for Abigail, Jacob, Zack, and Bo in their next Blast to the Past adventure, *Washington's War.*

Come visit us online at:

www.BlastToThePastBooks.com

Title: *Benjamin Franklin, Printer,* ca. 1928 by John Ward Dunsmore, oil on canvas, 28 x 36 inches

Collection of The New-York Historical Society. Accession Number 1938.312

The artist John Ward Dunsmore lived from 1856 to 1945. He is known for creating historically accurate paintings such as this one of Ben Franklin and his printing press.

BENJAMIN FRANKLIN TIME LINE

1706 Born in Boston on January 17, the youngest of seventeen children

1715 Finishes second and final year of formal school
Works in father's candle- and soap-making shop
Learns a love of exercise and begins weight lifting

1717 Invents a pair of swim fins for his hands

1718 Apprenticed to his brother James, a printer

1722 Under the pseudonym of Silence Dogood, writes a series of letters for James's newspaper

1723 Leaves apprenticeship, runs away to Philadelphia, and is employed as a printer

1729 Purchases and runs the *Pennsylvania Gazette*

1731 Set up the first lending library in the country

1732 Publishes the first edition of *Poor Richard's Almanack* under the pseudonym Richard Saunders

1736 Organizes the Union Fire Company

1737 Appointed postmaster of Philadelphia and, out of concern for delivery distances, invents an odometer

1741 Creates the Franklin Stove (a pipe stove)

1747 Writes the first political cartoon published in America
Writes as Miss Polly Baker about the injustices of being a single mother

1750 Invents the lightning rod

1752 Conducts the famous kite experiment, proving that there is only one kind of electrical current

1762 Invents the glass armonica, a simple musical instrument

1764 Charts the Gulf Stream

1776 Signs the Declaration of Independence

1778 Negotiates and signs the Treaty of Alliance with France

1782 Negotiates and signs the Paris Pact, a peace treaty with Great Britain

1784 Invents bifocals
Proposes daylight savings time plan

1785 Invents a clawlike instrument for taking books down from a high shelf
Discusses methods for keeping hold of a ship watertight

1787 Signs the United States Constitution

1790 Dies in Philadelphia on April 17, at the age of 84

Calling all junior detectives!

Do you like to solve mysteries?
If the answer is yes, then Nancy Drew needs you!

Can you help Nancy and her friends crack these cases?

THIRD-GRADE DETECTIVES

Everyone in the third grade loves the new teacher, Mr. Merlin.

Mr. Merlin used to be a spy, and he knows all about secret codes and the strange and gross ways the police solve mysteries.

YOU CAN HELP DECODE THE CLUES AND SOLVE THE MYSTERY IN THESE OTHER STORIES ABOUT THE THIRD-GRADE DETECTIVES:

#1 The Clue of the Left-handed Envelope
#2 The Puzzle of the Pretty Pink Handkerchief
#3 The Mystery of the Hairy Tomatoes
#4 The Cobweb Confession
#5 The Riddle of the Stolen Sand
#6 The Secret of the Green Skin
#7 The Case of the Dirty Clue
#8 The Secret of the Wooden Witness
#9 The Case of the Sweaty Bank Robber
#10 The Mystery of the Stolen Statue

ALADDIN PAPERBACKS • Simon & Schuster Children's Publishing • www.SimonSaysKids.com

Ready-for-Chapters

Read all the books in the

Blast to the Past™

series!

#1 Lincoln's Legacy

#2 Disney's Dream

#3 Bell's Breakthrough

#4 King's Courage

#5 Sacagawea's Strength

#6 Ben Franklin's Fame

Coming Soon:

#7 Washington's War